PUFFIN

DRAGON RIDE

Helen Cresswell was born in Nottingham and educated there and at King's College, London. She now lives in Robin Hood country. She spent most of her childhood writing books for adults, and is now spending her adulthood writing books for children. She has now written over one hundred books, many of which have been televised. Her hobbies are collecting antiques (she hopes eventually to become one herself), painting, walking in the country and exploring new places.

Helen Cresswell
Dragon Ride

Illustrated by Ruth Rivers

PUFFIN BOOKS

PUFFIN BOOKS

Published by the Penguin Group
Penguin Books Ltd, 80 Strand, London, WC2R 0RL, England
Penguin Group (USA), Inc., 375 Hudson Street, New York, New York 10014, USA
Penguin Books Australia Ltd, Ringwood, Victoria, Australia
Penguin Books Canada Ltd, 10 Alcorn Avenue, Toronto, Ontario, Canada M4V 3B2
Penguin Books India (P) Ltd, 11 Community Centre, Panchsheel Park, New Dehli – 110 0117, India
Penguin Group (NZ), cnr Airborne and Rosedale Roads, Albany, Auckland 1310, New Zealand
Penguin Books (South Africa) (Pty) Ltd, 5 Watkins Street, Denver Ext 4, Johannesburg 2094, South Africa

On the World Wide Web at: www.penguin.com

Penguin Books Ltd, Registered Offices: Harmondsworth, Middlesex, England

First published by Viking 1997
Published in Puffin Books 1989
Published in this edition 1999
13

Printed in Singapore by Star Standard
Typeset in 15/22 Times New Roman

British Library Cataloguing in Publication Data
A CIP catalogue record for this book is available from the British Library

ISBN 13: 978-0-14130-290-4

Chapter One

All Jilly wanted in the world was a dragon. Luckily, it was her birthday next month. She would be seven.

She told her brother, Ben. She didn't really think he could afford a dragon (he was only five), but she asked him anyway.

"What – one that puffs fire?" he asked her.

"Yes," replied Jilly. "One that puffs *lots* of fire. Not at everybody, mind you. Just at the people I *want* it to puff at."

She already had a long list of people who would get scorched if she got her dragon.

"How do I know it wouldn't puff at me?" Ben asked. "*I'm* not getting you a dragon. I'm getting you –"

"Shush!" Jilly shrieked. "Shush! Don't tell!"

Ben clapped his hand to his mouth. If you had a secret, Ben was the last person in the world that you told it to. He had just nearly given away his own secret!

Jilly had always secretly thought how marvellous it would be to have a dragon as a pet. She loved the look of them. She loved their shiny green scales and curly tails. And on most pictures she had ever seen of dragons, they seemed to be smiling. Even when they were puffing out great clouds of smoke and fire, there always seemed to be that faint, secret smile.

Dragons, she knew, didn't grow on trees. In fact, up till now, she had thought it was impossible to get a dragon at all. Then she saw something about them in her comic. It told you about people who keep them as pets. It told you what to

feed them on, and how often to take them for walks. Jilly cut out the page and kept it carefully at the back of her stamp album.

Jilly asked for the dragon when the family was sitting round having dinner.

"It's all I want in the world!" she said.

"That'd be handy," said Mr Tonks. "No need to buy another box of matches ever again!"

"Now come along, Arthur," said Mrs Tonks. "Don't tease the child."

"Fry the bacon on its breath," went on Mr Tonks. "Just think of that!"

"I'm not joking, Dad," said Jilly. "I really, really want a dragon. I

don't want any other presents. In fact, if I can have a dragon, I don't even mind not getting any presents next Christmas, either."

"It's easy to say that in April," her mother said. "You wait until December, and *then* see if you don't care about Christmas presents."

"*Please*, Mum," said Jilly. "I mean it."

"If you ask me," said Mrs Tonks, "there are no such things as dragons. I've never seen one in a zoo."

"Well, you wouldn't, would you?" said Jilly. "They'd escape. They'd just melt the bars of their

cages with their fire, and fly off."

"Can they fly?" asked Mrs Tonks. "Where do dragons come from, then? Are they hatched out of eggs, in a nest? Anyway, I'm sure we can't afford to buy one, Jilly, let alone feed it. You'd best forget all about it. What else would you like for your birthday?"

"It's Saturday today," said Jilly. "We'll be going into town. Won't you please even *ask* about a dragon?"

"Just think, Mary," said Mr Tonks to his wife. "If we had a dragon, we could sell the car. We could fly everywhere on its back. And there'd be no trouble about parking ever again!"

"Oooh!" cried Ben. "I'd like that!"

"Be quiet, Arthur," Mrs Tonks told her husband. "I'm sorry, Jilly, but we shan't get you a dragon. I told you – I'm not even sure that there *are* such things. They're just in stories, not in real life."

"That's what *I* thought," Jilly

said. "And then I saw something in my comic. Wait – I'll go and get it."

She ran and fetched the cutting from the back of her stamp album.

"Here!" she said. "Read this!"

As Mrs Tonks read it she looked more and more surprised.

"Fancy that!" she said. "People *do* have them as pets, then. It tells you what to give them to eat, to make them puff a lot of fire. Well, fancy! It doesn't say anything about how much they cost, though."

"Give it to me, Mary," said Mr Tonks.

He read it too. Then he began to laugh. He laughed so much that tears ran down his face. He laughed so much that he could hardly speak.

"Oh, dear!" he gasped at last, wiping his eyes. "Oh, dear!"

"What's so funny?" demanded Jilly.

"Are you laughing or crying, Dad?" asked Ben.

"Oh, Mary! To think that you believed every word of it!" said Mr Tonks.

"Of course I did!" said his wife, quite huffily. "It's in Jilly's comic. Why shouldn't I believe it?"

"And me!" cried Jilly. "I believe it!"

"Ah, but you're only six," he told her. "You couldn't be expected to notice."

"Notice what?" asked Mrs Tonks.

"The *date*, Mary," he told her. "Look, at the top of the page. 1 April!"

He held it out, and Jilly and her mother both stared.

"April Fool's Day," he said. "You were made an April Fool, the pair of you!"

Jilly could have cried. She snatched the comic away from her father and screwed it up into a ball. She ran to the bin and pushed it in.

"Stupid!" she said. "Stupid comic!"

"Now come along, Jilly," said her mother. "It was only a joke. Surely you can take a joke?"

But Jilly could not take this particular joke. After reading that comic she had set her heart on having a dragon. Even if she didn't have one for her birthday, she had

meant to buy one for herself. She
would have saved up for years, if
she had to.

And now it looked as if there
were no such things as dragons
after all. Suddenly the world seemed
a very dull and empty place.

"Well, if there aren't such things
as dragons, there *ought* to be!" she

cried, and ran out of the room.

In her bedroom she stared at the poster of a dragon on the wall.

"I believe in you," she told him. "I *still* believe in you!"

And the painted dragon seemed to smile a little more widely than usual.

"Listen," she told him. "I'm

going out for a while. I'll be back soon. And when I *do* get back, I may have a surprise for you. I may have a surprise for everybody!"

She unlocked the tin where she kept her savings and took out some money.

"Wait there!" she told the dragon, and went back downstairs.

"Please may I come with you into town?" she asked.

Everybody thought she had forgotten all about the dragon.

··· Chapter Two ···

And so the Tonkses all set off into town. Jilly knew exactly where she was going. Luckily, Ben had to go and try on new shoes.

"Can I go to the Magic Shop while you're looking for shoes?" asked Jilly.

"*I* want to come!" cried Ben

immediately, as Jilly knew he
would.

"I'll go with you, Jilly," said Mr
Tonks.

So Jilly and her father went off
together.

"Can you wait outside the shop
while I go in?" Jilly asked. She
wanted to ask for something very

special indeed, and she didn't want anyone to hear her.

"Oh, I'll be happy enough outside, just looking in the window," her father said.

They both stopped outside the Magic Shop, and looked in the window. Jilly could spend hours doing that. She thought that if she had a thousand pounds she could spend every penny of it there.

Her father must have read her thoughts.

"I used to spend half my pocket-money here, when I was your age," he told Jilly.

She gazed at the masks of clowns, monsters and witches. She gazed at the conjuring tricks, invisible ink, stink-bombs and other delights. She wished she could have them all. For a time, she forgot why she had come.

Then she remembered. She took a deep breath, pushed open the door and went in. Her father poked his head into the shop and called:

"Morning, Mr Pink! Not allowed in today, Jilly tells me!"

"Good morning, Arthur."

The door closed. It was dim in there, and had an exciting smell of magic. Mr Pink, who owned the shop, was behind the counter, wearing a red fez. (He wore a

different hat every day, and
sometimes he wore masks, beards,
false noses or ears.)

He smiled at Jilly. He knew her
well, as he had known her father
before her. He was old and his face
was very crinkled and lined.

"What can I do for you today?"

he asked. "A disappearing snake, perhaps, or a talking mouse?"

Jilly took another deep breath.

"Please, Mr Pink, today I'd like some – some *real* magic!"

He looked at her then, long and hard.

"Of course," he said at last.

"Why else would you come here?"

"I want a dragon," Jilly told him. "I know you can't buy them, but I'm sure there *are* such things. I know it in my bones."

"If you believe in dragons," said Mr Pink, "then of course there are such things – for *you*."

He did not sound at all surprised. He behaved as if someone asked him for a dragon every day of the week.

"Was there any particular kind of dragon you had in mind?" he went on.

"Oh, yes, yes!" Jilly told him eagerly. "I'd like one just like the one on the poster in my bedroom. One with bright green scales and a

curly tail. He's puffing out fire, but he looks really tame. He's smiling. I'm sure he is."

"Well, then, you shall have that very one," Mr Pink told her.

"Really?" cried Jilly. "You mean – you mean you can bring him to life?"

Mr Pink did not reply. He fetched a pair of stepladders and placed them against the shelves. Then he climbed up, right to the very top.

"Let me see, let me see . . ." she heard him mutter.

Jilly saw him take a small box from the very back of that mysterious top shelf. Then, very carefully, he came down again.

"What a lot of cobwebs!" he said. "What a lot of dust! I don't get asked for real magic every day, you see."

Jilly glanced quickly towards the

window, to make sure her father was not peeping. Luckily he was still looking at the masks and tricks in the window.

Mr Pink took the large green handkerchief from his top pocket and carefully dusted the box. Jilly could see that it was very, very old. It was made of wood, and strange signs and letters were carved on it.

"And now," he said to Jilly, "it's time for secrets!"

When Jilly left the shop she had a small green packet in one hand and her money in the other. Mr Pink would not take any money.

"Oh, no!" he said. "This is real magic. No money must change hands, or it won't work. And you

cannot come back for more. This is
once and once only magic. Now,
keep the spell in your left hand and
the money in your right until you
get home!"

Outside the shop Mr Tonks took one look at her smile.

"It looks as though you got what you wanted," he told her.

"Yes," Jilly told him, and smiled the more. But not another word did they say. *She* knew how to keep secrets, even if Ben didn't.

When she got home Jilly put her money back in the box, and hid the tiny green packet under her pillow.

"Just you wait!" she whispered to the dragon on the wall.

Chapter Three

Usually, Ben went to bed an hour earlier than Jilly, because he was younger. But tonight, Jilly said,

"I'd like to go to bed when Ben does tonight. I'm tired."

This was because of what Mr Pink had said to her when he gave her the spell.

"It will work only in the hour between day and night. It will work only at dawn, or at dusk."

Jilly could not bear to wait until the next day. Besides she might be fast asleep and not wake up at dawn. At seven o'clock she went upstairs.

"Just you wait!" she whispered

again to her dragon on the wall as
she changed into her pyjamas.
"You and I are going for a ride!"

She went into Ben's room. He
was already in bed.

"Good-night," she said. "Sweet
dreams!"

"Sweet dreams you as well,
Jilly!" he said. He had said this

every night since the time when he
was first learning to talk. Tonight,
she thought, her adventures would
be dreams come *true*.

Jilly went and climbed into bed.
Her mother came in to kiss her

good-night. Jilly wondered what she would say if she knew that there was a spell under the pillow?

Jilly waited for five minutes and then got out of bed. She lifted the pillow and took out the tiny green package. She carried it over to her table. Then she went to take down her dragon poster. Her fingers were trembling. She carried the poster over to the table and stared down at it.

She had lain in bed and gazed at it so many times before that she knew every tiny detail. If she closed her eyes, she could still see it.

What was it Mr Pink had said?

"First, you must name him."

Jilly had thought about this all

day. She touched the painted dragon lightly on the head.

"I name you Lancelot!" she told him. He did not stir. He was still fixed and painted on the paper. She was pleased with the name. She thought it sounded good and dragon-like. You couldn't give a dragon an ordinary name like John or Mark or Keith.

Now came the most important moment of all. She opened the tiny parcel and stared at the pale green powder. Then, very carefully, she repeated to herself the words Mr Pink had told her to say.

"I take you, Lancelot, to be my dream," she whispered. "We will go invisible, like the wind!"

She waited, breath held, eyes still tight shut. Could it be, could it possibly be that, at this very moment, a real dragon was unfurling real wings from the flat prison of the poster?

She thought she felt a stir of the air, a faint breath against her

cheek. Half eager and half afraid
she opened her eyes.

"Oh!" she gasped.

There was the dragon she had
longed for and dreamed of. His
green scales glittered, his eyes were
bright and black. Best of all, he was
smiling.

"Lancelot!" she breathed. "You're really real!"

"Of course I am," the dragon replied. "Thanks to you. How stiff I am!"

He stretched himself. His wings spread. His tail lashed.

"Can you – can you puff fire?" she asked him. She added hastily, "Please don't scorch anything! Perhaps we'd better wait till we're outside. You will let me ride on your back, won't you?"

"I have come for that very purpose," he told her. "Are you brave enough? Won't you be frightened to be on a dragon's back and high in the air?"

"Of course not!" cried Jilly. "I can hardly wait! Can we go now?"

"We have only one hour," said Lancelot. "And the minutes are already ticking by. Open the window! How I've longed to see what lies beyond!"

"Have you really?" Jilly was

surprised. "Could you see, then, and could you think, when you were –" She stopped short. She hardly liked to say, "when you were only a poster". It sounded somehow rather rude.

She ran to the window and opened it wide.

"Now climb on my back!" commanded Lancelot. "You may hold on to the spines on my neck."

Jilly obeyed. His scales and spines were smooth and cold. She shivered.

"Ready?" he asked.

"Ready!" she replied. Her voice trembled.

··· Chapter Four ···

And then they were off! She felt the strong upward beat of his wings as he soared through the window and into the open air.

She looked down, and saw the garden below. She saw the roses, the apple trees and her father, digging. She gave a gasp. What if he looked up, and saw her?

"We are invisible, remember," came Lancelot's voice. It was as if he read her thoughts.

"So we are!" She felt suddenly free. "Hurrah! We can go where we like, and no one will see us. Puff some fire! Please puff some fire!"

Lancelot obeyed. It was just as

she had dreamed it would be.
Flames went forking out on all
sides. They danced and curled like
scarlet snakes.

"Hurrah!" Jilly yelled again.

"What about some green
smoke?" he called.

"Oh yes, please! Puff some green
smoke! Puff lots of it!"

And so he did. Now the scarlet

snakes were dancing in a green
mist.

As the dragon rose higher and
higher, Jilly could see tiny people
walking below. They looked like
toys.

"If they looked up, all they'll see
is the moon coming up," Jilly
thought.

They could not guess that right
above their very heads was a
dragon flying.

"There's my school!" she cried.
"Fly over my school!"

And so he did. Jilly looked down
on the roof, and on the playground.

"School will never seem the same
again!" she thought.

"What if I go to school on

Monday and tell Miss Barker about tonight? She'd never believe it. She'd think it was just a dream, or a story I'd made up."

Jilly laughed aloud at the thought.

"Higher!" she cried. "More fire! More smoke!"

Lancelot obeyed. He seemed to enjoy puffing the flames and the smoke as much as Jilly enjoyed seeing them. After all, he had spent his life as a prisoner in a poster until now.

Now they were over the river. Lancelot flew down until they were quite low over the silvery water. Families on the banks were packing up their picnics, ready to go home. It was growing darker, minute by minute.

All at once, the people started waving.

"They can see us!" cried Jilly, and she waved back. She was proud

to be seen riding a dragon. She felt
like a queen.

"Puff lots more flames and
smoke!" she yelled, and Lancelot
obeyed.

"Look, Jilly!" he called. "A
boat!"

Jilly looked. Sure enough, a boat
was moving slowly down the silvery
river. The people were waving at the

boat, not at themselves at all.

Jilly stopped waving. She felt rather silly to be waving at nothing.

"Fancy waving at a boat!" she called to Lancelot. "Fancy waving at a boat when they could have waved at a dragon!"

"If they saw us, it would mean that the spell was wearing off," he replied.

So Jilly was glad that they were not waving at her.

For a whole hour the two of them rode above the town. They dipped and dived and made patterns in the air. Jilly turned to see their trail of fire and sparks and green smoke.

Then lights began to twinkle below them. Jilly could see the pale circle of the moon. Lancelot turned back the way he had come.

"Oh no!" cried Jilly. "It can't be the end of my ride! An hour can't have gone already!"

But it had. And the world of magic has its own laws, just as the real world has. Soon they were over Jilly's garden again, where Mr Tonks was just putting away his spade.

"Ooooeeeh!" cried Jilly as Lancelot flew right through her open window. She felt a soft bump. Blinking, she looked about her. She was lying on her bed. Over on the table lay the dragon poster.

"Oh, Lancelot!" She got up and ran to him. He lay fixed and painted. He still smiled. But was his smile . . . perhaps . . . just a little wider . . . ?

She touched his painted head.

"Thank you, Lancelot," she whispered. "You made my dream come true."

And then she got into bed.

One thing is certain. That was not Jilly's last ride. After that, she would sometimes whisper to her painted dragon before she went to bed.

"I take you, Lancelot, to be my dream. We will go invisible, like the wind!"

And sure enough, she and

Lancelot would fly away. They would fly all night sometimes over the sleeping town, both of them sharing the same dream.

And for her birthday, Jilly had a bicycle. She could have a bicycle ride by day, and by night a dragon ride.

So now Jilly has the best of both worlds.